THE INTERGALACTIC NEMESIS

BOOK ONE: TARGET EARTH

THE INTERGALACTIC NEMESIS

BOOK ONE: TARGET EARTH

Written by
Jason Neulander

Pencils & Inks by
Tim Doyle

Color Art by
Paul Hanley and Lee Duhig

Lettering by
Tim Doyle and Doug Dlin

THANKS TO

Buzz Moran, Graham Reynolds, Etta Sanders, Derek Rosenstrauch, Molly Rice, Japhy Fernandez, (The Real) Ben Willcott, John Weiss, Tony Nozaro, Lindsay Doleshal, Corey Gagne, Dan Dietz, David Sangalli, Ben Anderson, John DeFore, Rachel Koper, Laura Phelan, Peter Stopschinski, Lee Eddy, Brent Werzner, Shannon McCormick, Mike D'Alonzo, David Higgins, LB Deyo, Christopher Lee Gibson, Shana Merlin, Mical Trejo, Jon Watson, Diana Duecker, Derek Menningen, Cynthia Patterson, Charles Leslie, Pebbles Wadsworth, Conrad Haden, The University of Texas Performing Arts Center, Christine Tschida, Rena Shagan, Seth Goldstein, The Splinter Group, Bill Hofstetter/Agency 212, Mammoth Advertising (NYC), Rob Nuell, Maria Quinn, Pam Lubell, Leanne Schanzer, Jeff Croiter, Jonathan Herzog, Jeremy Lee, Robert Fried, Neil Patel, Bridget Klapinski, Carter Jackson, Robert Faires, The Austin Chronicle, KUT-FM, Ratgirl, Cliff and Cynthia Chapman, Adam Russell, Marc Seriff, Cord Shiflet, Scott Reichardt, Sarah André, Piper and Scarlett, and the thousands of people who've seen and loved the show since its inception back in 1996.

---

www.theintergalacticnemesis.com

Inquiries:
The Robot Planet
2318 Canterbury St
Austin, TX 78702
jason@theplanetzygon.com

CHAPTER ONE

Mystery at Kradmoor

In which we meet Pulitzer-winner *Molly Sloan*, her intrepid
assistant *Timmy Mendez*, the world-famous mesmerist *Mysterion
the Magnificent*, and a *mysterious stranger* with the skinny on the
STORY OF THE CENTURY.

1933.
SOMEWHERE IN THE CARPATHIAN
MOUNTAINS OF EASTERN EUROPE.

THERE'S SOMETHING ODD HERE, MOLLY.

ODD LIKE THE NUMBER *THIRTEEN*, KID.

MY MOTHER *PASSED AWAY* WHEN I WAS *FOUR*,

BUT LORD CRAWFORD DIDN'T EVEN *BAT AN EYE* WHEN I TOLD HIM MY *MOTHER* SAID *HELLO*.

WOAH! YOU THINK THIS HAS SOMETHING TO DO WITH THAT *MYSTERIOUS STRANGER'S* STRANGE WARNING BACK IN *TRANSYLVANIA?*

I DON'T KNOW, KID, BUT YOU CAN BET YOUR OLD MAN'S *PIG FARM* I'M GOING TO *FIND OUT!*

YOUR *ROOMS*.

SEE YOU AT THE *PARTY*, KID. AND, HEY, SPIT OUT THAT *TAFFY*, WILL YOU?

ALL RIGHT, MISS SLOAN.

IS THIS PARTY *REALLY* BEING HELD...

...*OUTSIDE??*

I HOPE MYSTERION *PICKS ME!*

ME TOO. IF YOU'RE *DISTRACTING* EVERYONE, I CAN *POKE AROUND THE CASTLE* AND FIND THE SOURCE OF LORD CRAWFORD'S SUDDEN *AMNESIA.*

YES, MR. MENDEZ! YOU WILL BE MY *FIRST SUBJECT!*

GOOD *LUCK,* KID!

YOU *TOO,* MOLLY.

COME TO THE *STAGE,* YOUNG MENDEZ!

NOW, MR. MENDEZ, YOU AND I HAVE *NEVER MET BEFORE,* IS THAT CORRECT?

UH, WELL, ACTUALLY, MR. MYSTERION, WHEN WE *GOT* TO THE *CASTLE,* YOU--

LOOK INTO MY *EYES!*

NO, WE HAVE *NEVER MET BEFORE,* MASTER MYSTERION.

CLAP CLAP CLAP CLAP CLAP CLAP CLAP CL

-*EXCELLENT* JOB, MR. MENDEZ. PLEASE, DON'T LEAVE THE *STAGE*.

...LADIES AND GENTLEMEN! YOU MAY HAVE NOTICED WE ARE *OUT OF DOORS*, SHELTERED BY A *LARGE CANVAS*.

THAT A *LIGHTNING STORM* RAGES OUTSIDE!

NOW, NOTICE CURTAIN RISING *BEHIND* ME!

...YOU MAY HAVE NOTICED THAT A *GIANT METAL ROD* JUTS OUT FROM THE *TOP OF THE TENT*.

BEHIND THAT CURTAIN SITS A DEVICE OF *UNSTOPPABLE POWER!*

...A *MESMER-MACHINE* DESIGNED TO *ENTRANCE* THIS ENTIRE ROOM!

...LADIES AND GENTLEMEN...

...BEHOLD...

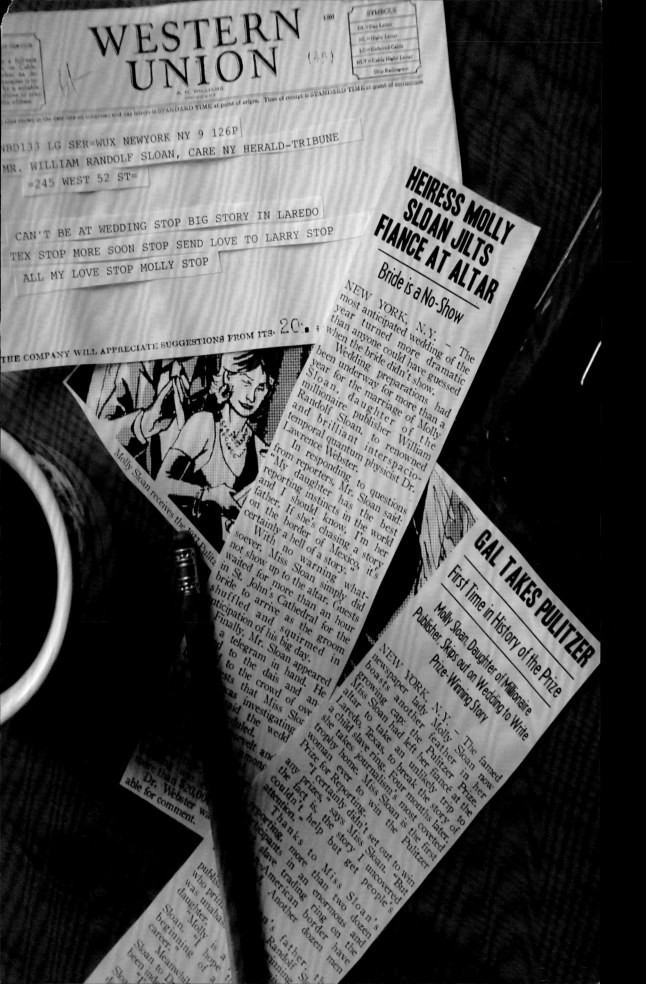

WESTERN UNION

A. N. WILLIAMS
PRESIDENT

SYMBOLS
DL = Day Letter
NL = Night Letter
LC = Deferred Cable
NLT = Cable Night Letter
Ship Radiogram

The filing time as shown in the date line on telegrams and day letters is STANDARD TIME at point of origin. Time of receipt is STANDARD TIME at point of destination

NBD133 LG SER=WUX NEWYORK NY 9 126P=

MR. WILLIAM RANDOLF SLOAN, CARE NY HERALD—TRIBUNE

=245 WEST 52 ST=

CAN'T BE AT WEDDING STOP BIG STORY IN LAREDO
TEX STOP MORE SOON STOP SEND LOVE TO LARRY STOP
ALL MY LOVE STOP MOLLY STOP

THE COMPANY WILL APPRECIATE SUGGESTIONS FROM ITS.

Molly Sloan receives the 1932 Pulitz

HEIRESS MOLLY SLOAN JILTS FIANCE AT ALTAR

Bride is a No-Show

NEW YORK, N.Y. — The most anticipated wedding of the year turned more dramatic than anyone could have guessed when the bride didn't show.

Wedding preparations had been underway for more than a year for the marriage of Molly Sloan, daughter of millionaire publisher William Randolf Sloan, to renowned and brilliant temporal quantum interspacio-temporal physicist Dr. Lawrence Webster.

In responding to questions from reporters, Mr. Sloan said: "My daughter has the best reporting instincts in the world and I should know, I'm her father. If she's chasing a story on the border of Mexico, it's certainly a hell of a story."

With no warning whatsoever, Miss Sloan simply did not show up to the altar. Guests waited for more than an hour in St. John's Cathedral for the bride to arrive as the groom shuffled and squirmed in anticipation of his big day. Finally, Mr. Sloan appeared a telegram in hand. He ___ to the dais and an___ to the crowd of ove___ ___as that Miss Slo___ ___as investigating ___ ___ the wedd___ ___led. ___oosevelt and ___ ___mon ___

more than $20,00___
Dr. Webster wa___
able for comment.

GAL TAKES PULITZER

First Time in History of the Prize

Molly Sloan, Daughter of Millionaire Publisher, Skips out on Wedding to Write Prize-Winning Story

NEW YORK, N.Y. — The famed newspaper lady, Molly Sloan boasts another feather in her growing cap: the Pulitzer Prize. Miss Sloan had left her fiancé at the altar to take an unlikely trip to Laredo, Texas, to break the story of a child slave ring. Four months later she takes journalism's most coveted trophy home. Miss Sloan is the first woman ever to win the Pulitzer Prize for Reporting.

"I certainly didn't set out to win any prizes," says Miss Sloan. "But the fact is the story I uncovered couldn't help but get people's attention."

Thanks to Miss Sloan's reporting, more than two dozen participants in an enormous and ___American border ___ trading ring on the ___ slave in an ___ ___than two dozen ___ Another dozen men ___

publis___
who prin___
was unaba___
daughter.
"Molly is ___
Sloan, "I hope ___
beginning of a ___
career."
Meanwhile ___
Sloan to D ___
been ind ___
Sloan ___

___n's father ___
___Randolf S___
___inning St___

SLAVE RING DISCOVERED ON MEXICO BORDER

Lost Children Reunited with Their Families

Factory Owners Implicated

by Molly Sloan

A child slave in Laredo just moments before he was freed.

LAREDO, Tex.–In this sleepy border town with its traditions of siestas and moonlight serenades, there exists a secret and seedy underbelly. While on the streets venders ply their wares and the occasional souse causes a ruckus, behind the walls of at least a dozen storefronts hundreds of children, thought dead, work deadly machines for a few crusts of bread a day. Yes, on this border of Texas and Mexico, where owning a slave was made a Federal crime more than 65 years ago by the 13th Amendment of the United States Constitution, slavery is alive and well.

It all would have remained a secret if not for the courage of one boy, Timmy Mendez, a child of migrant farm workers who exceeded all hope by graduating from Harvard University and who blew the whistle on this crime against humanity.

In two countries

It appears as if slavery never disappeared in this part of the country, so far from the authorities in Washington D.C. and in a state known for its wild ways and corruption. The Texas capitol building grounds in Austin prominently feature several memorials honoring the soldiers of the Confederacy who defended slavery and it is clear that those Texan "traditions" never truly went away.

Working in textile factories, metal shops, and farm equipment manufacturers, hundreds of brown-skinned children, as young as age 6, literally slave away for twelve, fourteen, sometimes sixteen hours a day building, sewing, and molding goods that are bought and sold across the United States every day. This reporter estimates that one in every five households in America owns at least one article touched by the hands of these young, innocent prisoners.

The crime crosses the border to Nuevo Laredo as well and the criminals perpetrating these crimes are of both American and Mexican nationalities. It appears as if none of the companies who contract with these factories were aware that the workers in them were slaves.

"I am outraged that we were duped by these criminals," says Mr. Owen Young, chairman of General Electric, one of the companies that has hired these illegal manufactories. "I sincerely hope the owners of these sweatshops are prosecuted to the full extent of the law."

Slavery plot

Starting in the 'teens, pa[...] had been reporting mi[...] children across nort[...] Mexico and Southwest [...] Since 1919, more tha[...] children have been re[...]

missing, yet not one had bee[...] recovered. The authorities ha[...] been under the payroll of th[...] slave owners and turned [...] blind eye to the horrible crime[...] Many parents finally assum[...] their children were dead.

More than a dozen facto[...] owners were part of the c[...] slave ring. They hired [...] men" to approach the child[...] after school or while th[...] parents were at work and [...] were home alone. Th[...] kidnappers would coax [...] children into their cars [...] such simple tactics as offe[...] candy. Then, once the [...] had entered the vehicle, [...] he was gagged wi[...] handkerchief dosed with [...] When they awakened, [...] often found themselves c[...] to a dangerous machin[...] told to work at it nig[...] day.

(continued on [...]

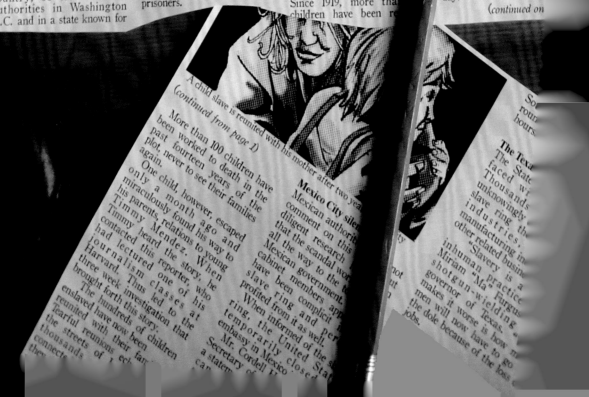

A child slave is reunited with his mother after two yea[...]

(continued from page 1)

More than 100 children have been worked to death in the past fourteen years of the plot, never to see their families again.

One child, however, escaped only a month ago and miraculously found his way to his parents, relations to young Timmy Mendez. When Timmy heard the story, he contacted this reporter, who had lectured one of his journalism classes at Harvard. Thus led to the three week investigation that brought forth this story.

The hundreds of children enslaved have now been reunited with their fam[...] the streets of [...] tearful reunions of [...] thousands of [...] connect[...]

Mexico City silen[...] Mexican authoriti[...] comment on this [...] diligent research [...] that the scandal wo[...] all the way to the t[...] Mexican government [...] have been complicit [...] cabinet members app[...] slave ring and pe[...] profited from it as well.

When informed of the s[...] ring, the United Stat[...] temporarily close[...] embassy in Mexico [...] Mr. Cordell [...] Secretary o[...] a statement [...] can[...]

So[...] roun[...] hours [...]

The Texa[...] The State [...] faced wi[...] Thousands [...] unknowingly[...] slave ring th[...] industries, [...] manufacturing in[...] other related busi[...] "Slavery is a [...] inhuman practice[...] Miriam "Ma" Furgu[...] shotgun-wielding [...] governor of Texas. "[...] makes it worse is how m[...] men will now have to go [...] the dole because of the loss [...] jobs.

CHAPTER TWO

Enter Stranger

In which Molly and Timmy find themselves at the mercy of Mysterion
and meet *Ben Wilcott*. Further mysteries at
Kradmoor are uncovered.

CASTLE KRADMOOR.
FALKIRK, SCOTLAND.

SORRY.
FORGOT MY
INVITATION.

OOF!

OH, NO,
YOU DON'T,
VILLAIN!

GET OFF THE
STAGE, YOU MEDDLING
INTERLOPER!

WHATEVER THEY
TOLD YOU IS A LIE,
MYSTERION!

HUMANS AND
ZYGONIANS CAN'T
COEXIST!

ONCE I ACTIVATE THE *CENTRAL HIVE* IN *TUNIS*, THE REST OF THE WORLD'S LEADERS WILL FALL UNDER MY SWAY...

...ENSURING MY *ABSOLUTE SUPREMACY* OVER THIS *ENTIRE GLOBE!*

MOLLY, THE *CENTRAL HIVE!* THAT *MAP!*

HUSH, TIMMY.

BUT *ENOUGH* ABOUT MY ITINERARY. WHO IS THE *SIMPERING APE* WHO *DESTROYED* MY *MESMOGRIFIER??!!*

I HAVE NO IDEA WHAT YOU'RE TALKING ABOUT, CREEPO!

REALLY? THAT'S NOT WHAT MY SOURCES IN *RUMANIA* TELL ME.

YOU! YOU'RE THE ONE WHO HAD *VLAD* KILLED!

THANKS TO YOU, WE HAD TO *SHUT DOWN* OUR BASE IN *TRANSYLVANIA!*

NO MATTER. SOON WE WILL BE OPERATING FROM *EVERY CORNER* OF THE GLOBE!

UH, MYSTERION, THE GLOBE IS A *SPHERE.* IT DOESN'T *HAVE* ANY *CORNERS!*

SHUT *UP*, MR. MENDEZ.

WHEN MY STORY *HITS THE PRESSES*, THE ONLY *BASE OF OPERATIONS* YOU'LL HAVE IS AN *8-BY-10 PRISON CELL!*

EMPTY THREATS, MY DEAR.

HAVE YOU *FORGOTTEN* THE *CIRCUMSTANCES* TO WHICH YOU ARE *CHAINED?*

CLICKCLICKCLICK

WHO IS YOUR ACCOMPLICE?!

LET ME **HELP** YOU **OUT** OF THAT THING.

THANK YOU... STRANGER.

OH, MY **LEGS.** THEY'RE LIKE **JELLY.**

DON'T WORRY. I'VE GOT YOU, MISS SLOAN.

oh.

well.

THANKS AGAIN, STRANGER. DO YOU WORK FOR **RESCUE INCORPORATED,** OR ARE YOU JUST **FREELANCE?**

SERIOUSLY, **THANKS,** MISTER, BUT JUST **WHO ARE YOU?**

I'M A **LIBRARIAN** FROM **FLAGSTAFF, ARIZONA,** BUT THAT'S NOT **IMPORTANT** RIGHT NOW.

THEY TEACH YOU HOW TO FIGHT LIKE THAT IN **LIBRARY SCHOOL?**

I BROUGHT YOU A **CHANGE OF CLOTHES,** MISS SLOAN. WE HAVE TO GET OUT OF HERE **NOW!**

THROUGH *HERE*. THE *COOK* SHOWED ME HOW TO DO THIS WHEN I WAS A *KID*.

SSKKRRRRSHH

AFTER YOU, MISS SLOAN.

SSKKRRRRSHH

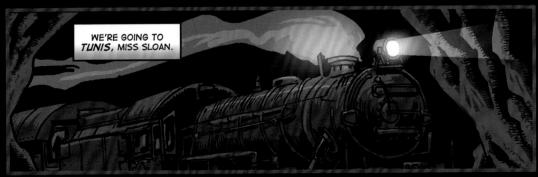

IT TOOK A WHILE, BUT I FOUND SOME GENUINE, *ALL-AMERICAN ATLANTIC CITY TAFFY*.

DID I MISS ANYTHING?

NOT HARDLY, KID. *RESCUE-BOY*, HERE, WAS JUST EXPLAINING HOW HE'S GOING TO *KNOCK OUT* THE *CENTRAL HIVE*.

MAYBE *THIS'LL* HELP.

WHAT'S THIS?

WE GOT IT FROM OUR CONTACT IN *TRANSYLVANIA*, BUT IT'S WRITTEN IN SOME KIND OF *CODE*.

LET ME SEE.

WHRRRRRR

WOW! WHAT'S WITH THAT *WRISTWATCH GIZMO?!*

YEAH, WHAT *IS* THAT THING, *DICK TRACY?*

IT'S AN *ALPHA-3 WRIST-TOP.*

WHRRRRRR

MOLLY...

I *KNOW*, KID, I *KNOW.*

JUST AS I *THOUGHT!* THIS ISN'T JUST A MAP, IT'S A *GROUND PLAN* OF THE *CENTRAL HIVE!*

YOU SEEM TO KNOW *A LOT* ABOUT THIS CENTRAL HIVE, MR. WILCOTT. THAT MUST BE SOME *LIBRARY* YOU HAVE IN *FLAGSTAFF.*

MISS SLOAN, MR. MENDEZ, I THINK IT'S TIME YOU KNEW THE TRUTH.

OH, BULLY! I *LOVE* A GOOD SECRET.

FASCINATING! I KNEW THERE WAS *MORE* TO THIS STORY! ARE YOU GETTING THIS *DOWN*, TIMMY?

BUT, MOLLY...

GET *SCRIBBLING*, KIDDO. THEY'LL PROBABLY GIVE ME SOME KIND OF *DOUBLE PULITZER* FOR THIS ONE.

ROGER, MOLLY. YOU CAN *COUNT ON ME.*

SPACE ALIENS, YOU SAY? OF COURSE. THERE CAN BE *NO OTHER EXPLANATION.* AND YOU SAY THEY'RE FROM *ZYGONIA?*

ZYGON, ACTUALLY. I KNOW IT MUST SOUND INCREDIBLE.

NO, WILCOTT. THIS IS THE FIRST THING YOU'VE SAID THAT *ACTUALLY MAKES SENSE.* AND THIS *CENTRAL HIVE?* THAT'S SOME SORT OF *SPACESHIP?*

NO, IT'S A KIND OF *NERVE CENTER.* THE ZYGONIANS WILL USE IT AS A *BASE OF OPERATIONS* WHEN THEIR MAIN FLEET ARRIVES IN *2095.*

DADDY WOULD LIKE THESE GUYS. THEY REALLY *PLAN AHEAD.*

SO YOU FOUND OUT ABOUT THE *INVASION,* AND NOW YOU'RE GOING TO TUNIS TO SAVE THE *WORLD.* WOW! WE'VE GOT A *REAL, LIVE HERO* ON OUR HANDS, MOLLY.

I'LL SAY. KIND OF A TALL ORDER FOR A *LIBRARIAN,* ISN'T IT, WILCOTT?

EACH OF US HAS A *DESTINY,* MOLLY, FOR *GOOD* OR FOR *EVIL.*

MY DESTINY STANDS *CLEARLY* BEFORE ME. IF IT TAKES *EVERY OUNCE OF LIFE* I HAVE IN ME, I WILL PUT AN *END* TO THE *ZYGONIAN TERROR,* ONCE AND FOR ALL.

I THINK I'LL SEE IF I CAN FIND A *NEWSPAPER*. EXCUSE ME.

GOOD GRIEF! THE POOR SAP'S GONE *BANANAS!*

TOO BAD. HE WAS STARTING TO LOOK KIND OF *CUTE.*

LOOK AT THIS...

YOU THINK HE'S *DANGEROUS*, MOLLY?

NO...

WESTERN UNION

NO RECORD OF BEN WILCOTT IN EMPLOY AT FLAGSTAFF PUBLIC LIBRARY STOP YOUR FRIENDS AT FPL STOP

...BUT ONE THING I *DO* KNOW...

IF *MYSTERION'S* GOING TO BE IN *TUNIS*, THAT'S WHERE THE *STORY* IS...

...AND I HAVE A *HUNCH* THIS WILCOTT'S GOING TO LEAD US *RIGHT TO IT.*

EXCUSE ME, MISS? COULD YOU HELP US WITH AN INQUIRY?

EXTRA!
MURDER IN SCOT
LORD MICHAEL
CRAWFORD FOUND
DEAD!

...AMERICAN REPORTER? ...FEMALE...?

YOU!

EXCUSE ME.

STOP!

GET HIM!

YOU ARE NOT GO-INK *NO-VHERE!*

THAT'S *ANYWHERE.* IF WE'RE NOT GOING *NOWHERE,* THAT MEANS WE'RE *REALLY* GOING *SOMEWHERE.*

BUT I SAID... VHAAAA??

AND THAT'S JUST MY *RIGHT,* TOUGH GUY!

VELL, I'LL BE UHHHHN...

C'MON, KID.

WE SHOULD BE ABLE TO *STAY WARM* IN HERE.

LOOKS LIKE THIS IS OUR *LUCKY DAY.* YOU *RIDE,* DON'T YOU, KID?

FOUR-TIME *GOAT ROPING CHAMP* OF ARMSTRONG COUNTY!

GREAT ARCHIVE! NOT A *HORSE.* ANYTHING BUT A *HORSE.*

WHAT'S THE MATTER, DOC?

HORSES. IT'S THEIR *EYES...*

...THEY *KNOW TOO MUCH!*

LOOK, I'M A CHAMPION *DRESSAGE RIDER* FROM MY *PREP SCHOOL* DAYS. YOU'LL BE *FINE...*

...JUST HOP ON AND HOLD TIGHT.

14 March, 1933 —

Last night, I played before King Geo. V and buffoon Ramsay MacDonald. What fool_____ are to allow me to perform before them. They have no comprehension of the scope of my powers, nor do they surmise my capacious ambition's yearnings. Unfortunately for them (yet fortunately for me) the show went over better than planned. I believe the Z— may be right — a global war that leaves me ruler of all mankind. Can it be? After all these years of planning? My childhood dream a reality? All will become much clearer at Kradmoor. My masters tell me that Lord Michael Crawford is no more. We shall see. Of course, they believe they have me under their control, but no one can control the master controller! Tonight! Tonight!

Naturally, my triumph in these next few days depends entirely on a working Mesmogrifier. With the help of the Z—, I was able to surprise the staff at Kradmoor with a test of that extraordinary device. It worked like a charm, especially that manservant called "Jeeves" (though I wonder if that is, indeed, his Christian name — no matter), he will make an excellent valet once my full plan has come to fruition. But the servants were surprised and my audience tonight shall certainly be more wary. (Can it really be tonight?? After all this time?) Nevertheless, that ingenious power coil was, indeed, just the piece of hardware I required. The Z— are truly masters of mind-control. I will certainly need to learn their secrets before I destroy them forever. Yes! Right now, I snicker inside. The Z— foolishly set at naught my own mental powers and this shall be their undoing.

It has been my great fortune to have been able to work in secret at our various operational bases. Bhutan, Transylvania (alas!), the North Pole, Eunis. What opportunity! Unsuspecting mind-slaves around the world awaiting the flick of the cerebral switch to be utterly at my beck and call, with no wills of their own! How long I have waited! But Eunis. Eunis. Therein lies the ultimate source of power! Eunis! I await thee...

CHAPTER THREE

Into the Mouth of the Beast

In which Molly, Timmy, and Ben arrive in Tunis in search of the CENTRAL HIVE. At a seedy bar they encounter the nefarious *Jean-Pierre Desperois* and Ben learns the true meaning of salt.

THIS *JEAN-PIERRE* DOESN'T SOUND LIKE SOMEONE--

TIMMY, DO YOU HAVE A *BETTER* IDEA?

NO, BUT--

JEAN-PIERRE HAS NO BETTER FRIENDS THAN *ANDREW JACKSON* AND *ULYSSES S. GRANT*...

...AND I KEEP THOSE FINE GENTLEMEN *CLOSE TO THE HEART* MYSELF.

ALL RIGHT, BOYS, THIS JOINT IS *PRETTY DANGEROUS*. KEEP YOUR *EYES PEELED*.

"*EYES PEELED*." I HAD *FORGOTTEN* ABOUT THAT ONE.

GENTLEMEN, I'M AFRAID WE WILL HAVE TO *CONTINUE* THIS CONVERSATION *ANOTHER TIME.*

BOYS, I'D LIKE YOU TO MEET *JEAN-PIERRE DESPEROIS.*

AH, MAM'SELLE SLOAN. SUCH A *BEAUTY* YOU ARE.

I SEE YOU ARE IN NEED OF MY...*SERVICES*... YET AGAIN...

KEEP YOUR *MITTS* OFF HER, *CREEP!*

WHO IS YOUR *LITTLE* FRIEND, MAM'SELLE SLOAN?

I'LL GIVE 'IM A *LESSON* ON BEING A *BIG MAN*, OUI?

ARE YOU *SURE* ABOUT THIS GUY?

NO.

WHAT'S THAT *WHITE POWDER* HE KEEPS POURING ON HIS *FOOD?*

THAT'S *SALT*, BEN. YOU EVER HEAR OF *SALT?*

BUT OF *COURSE*. LE *SALT*, SHE IS LE MOST *TASTY*. I CAN GET YOU AS *MUCH* AS YOU *LIKE*...

...FOR A *PRICE!*

ZHIS IS 'OW WE *FUND* OUR LITTLE *ORGANIZATION*, NON?

WE TRADE IN *SALT*, FROM LE MINES OF *TAOUDENNI*. BUT YOU ARE A *STRANGE* ONE, NON, TO NEVER *TASTE* LE *TASTE* OF LE *SALT!*

STRANGE? YOU'VE GOT A GIFT FOR *UNDERSTATEMENT*, JEAN-PIERRE.

NOW LET'S GET DOWN TO IT. WHAT HAVE YOU HEARD ABOUT THIS *CENTRAL HIVE?*

MY, 'OW YOU SAY, *MEMORY*, SHE IS *NOT SO GOOD* THESE DAYS, EH?

MAYBE THESE *OLD FRIENDS* OF YOURS'LL *REMIND* YOU.

AH, OUI, LE *CENTRAL 'IVE*. I BELIEVE I 'AVE *'EARD MENTION* OF SUCH A THING.

BUT *FIRST*, ANOZHER *WHISKEY*, NON?

I THINK YOU'VE HAD *ENOUGH*.

YOU THINK *SO?* 'OW 'BOUT I *CRUSH* YOU WIS MY *THUMB*, EH?

TRY ME, *JACKAL!*

THAT'S *ENOUGH!*

JEAN-PIERRE, I'LL BUY YOU AN *ENTIRE KEG* OF WHISKEY IF YOU GET US TO THIS CENTRAL HIVE.

YOU 'AVE FOR YOU, AS YOU *AMERICANS* LIKE TO SAY, A *DEAL*, NON? FOLLOW ME...

YOU WILL MEET YOUR *DEATH* SOON!

WHAT?

SQUAWK! YOU WILL DIE *LATER TODAY!* IN A TERRIBLE ACCIDENT. *SQUAWK!*

JUST *IGNORE* HIM. HE SAYS THAT TO *EVERYONE.*

'ERE IS THE PLACE WHERE LES MANY *STRANGENESSES* ARE, WHERE LES *EMPTY ONES* GO...

...L'ENTRANCE TO ZHE '*IVE,* SHE IS '*IDDEN* IN LE *BACK* OF LE *SHOP,* BUT TO *GET* ZHERE...

...YOU MUST MAKE PAST LE *SHOPKEEPER*...

...'E IS A *CLEVER* MAN...

...A *DANGEROUS* MAN...

THANKS, JEAN-PIERRE. YOU GOT *ANYTHING ELSE* FOR US?

I MUST GO. I BELIEVE I 'AVE A *KEG* OF *WHISKEY* WAITING FOR ME, NON? GOOD LUCK.

GOODBYE.

GOOD *RIDDANCE*.

ALL RIGHT. MR. WILCOTT, YOU AND I ARE *GOING IN FIRST*.

TIMMY, WAIT *THREE MINUTES*, THEN GO *AROUND BACK* AND FIND THAT *SECRET ENTRANCE*.

WHAT DO YOU HAVE IN *MIND*?

WE'RE GOING *RUG SHOPPING*, MR. WILCOTT.

UH--

WHY DO YOU ASK?

I'M TOLD THAT A BEAUTIFUL ⋺HEH⋸ *AMERICAN REPORTER* NAMED *MOLLY SLOAN* MIGHT BE HEADED THIS WAY...

...AND YOU JUST HAPPEN TO FIT THAT ⋺HEH⋸ *DESCRIPTION.*

THAT'S NOT *US.* WE'RE...

...*NEWLYWEDS* ON OUR *HONEYMOON.*

WE *ARE?*

OOF!

I MEAN, *YES, WE ARE.*

OKAY, YOU TWO. I WAS ABLE TO *DIG SOMETHING UP* BACK *HERE.*

LOOKS LIKE AN *ORDINARY BOOKCASE,* RIGHT?

BUT IF I TAKE *THIS...*

...AND PUT IT *HERE...*

HOW ON *EARTH...?*

THE KID'S A *WHIZ,* MR. WILCOTT.

UGH. WHAT'S THAT *STENCH?*

THAT'S *ZYGONIANS.* I FORGOT TO MENTION, THEY'RE A *SLUDGE-BASED,* LIFE FORM.

THE SLUDGE RESIDUE'LL BE *EVERYWHERE.* DON'T *TOUCH* IT.

THAT STUFF'LL *BURN* RIGHT THROUGH YOUR *SKIN.*

AFTER *YOU,* BOYS.

ALL RIGHT, TIMMY. YOU'VE GOT THE *PEARL*. LEAD ON.

I'M NOT SURE--

TIMMY...

OKAY.

DO YOU *HEAR* THAT, YOU TWO?

SSHHHHHHHAAA

IS IT... *VOICES?*

IS SOMEONE *DOWN* THERE?

DON'T *LISTEN* TO IT. IT'S THE *HIVE*. ZYGONIAN *MIND-CONTROL*. JUST KEEP *WALKING*.

HHHHHAAAAASSHHHHHHAAAAFFFOOOLLAAAASSSHHHH

GEEZ. SO, HOW ARE YOU PLANNING ON *FOULING UP* THIS CENTRAL HIVE *DO-HICKEY*, ANYWAY?

I...I'M *NOT SURE*, TIMMY. I DON'T EVEN KNOW WHAT A CENTRAL HIVE *LOOKS* LIKE.

DOES IT LOOK LIKE *THAT?!*

HHHHHAAAAASSHHHHHHHAAAAFFFOOOLLAAAASSSHHHH

WANTED - FOR SMUGGLING

Jean-Pierre Desperois AKA Jean-Pierre Desparois AKA Le Sel

DESCRIPTION

Age, mid-40s; height, 6 feet, four
inches, bare feet; weight, 250 pounds;
Skin, negroid; Hair, black; Eyes, brown;
Scars and marks, large scar on abdomen,
beard

RELATIVES

Unknown

(handwritten: Everytime we have him he disappears why???)

(handwritten: WHY KNOWN WHEREABOUTS? DOCKS OF TUNIS MARCHE LAFAYETTE MUST PUT OUT 24-HOUR WATCH)

CRIMINAL RECORD

Criminal record and fingerprints can be
obtained through Tunis Police,
Identification Order No. 1211, Issued
October 24, 1932.

Jean-Pierre Desperois is known to be armed and dangerous
He is an internationally wanted salt smuggler, purportedly us
the proceeds to fund a criminal operation resisting the Frenc
governm___ in Algeria.

opera___ no direct evidence has linked him to this
He is also ___as been seen and photographed with known rebels.
Toudenni, fr___ed for bribery in relation to the salt mines of
maintains a s___ich he obtains his black market salt. Desperois
out stores his ___led "safe house" in Tunis, capital of Tunisia,
farmers througho___gal salt stashes in the homes of peasant
Desperois ___isc___ Africa.
If apprehe___ ___nked to gun smuggling in the region.
___vestigation, a___ase notify the Director, Division of
the Special Agent in Charge of the office of the Division of
___vestigation listed on the back hereof which is nearest your
___y or town.

MURDER IN SCOTLAND

Lord Michael Crawford Found Dead

Mass Amnesia at Crime Scene

FALKIRK, Scotland – It was a scene of mass chaos. Scores of celebrities and diplomats wandering aimlessly over the grounds of Castle Kradmoor, the 30-acre ancestral home of the Crawford family. One man was dead on his birthday.

The body of Lord Michael Crawford, a distant relative of King George V, had been found mutilated in the subterranean levels of the castle, once the dungeons hundreds of years ago.

On the surface, spread across the marshlands and into the mountains, the guests of what had been Lord Crawford's birthday party were walking without purpose. All of them to a man had no memory of the past 72 hours.

It was the biggest case of mass amnesia on record.

"It was like a scene from one of those awful pulp science fiction novels my twelve-year-old son reads," said Constable Macdonaugh of Falkirk's local police department. "Mindless zombies everywhere, a corpse in the dungeon. But it's real. This time it's real!"

Authorities have no suspects yet in the murder. Scotland Yard has been called to further investigate.

"We are convinced that at least one guest saw the crime," said Yard Inspector Harlan Wallace.

The scene was utter chaos. More than 100 people had wandered throughout the estate. Famed actor Clark Gable was found unclothed, covered in mud next to a creek. A representative from the German Consulate was discovered clucking like a chicken while hopping on one foot in the Crawford family graveyard.

No one on the scene could explain what was going on.

Scotland Yard flew renowned Austrian psychiatrist Dr. Sigfried Roy from his mental ward in Vienna to the scene of the crime in an effort to solve the series of mysteries.

"Perhaps an astronomical phenomenon?" said Dr. Roy. "It is simply to early to say. I may have some answers after we study these poor people. But right now? We can only guess."

"We would like to talk with the stage magician who was supposed to perform here," said Inspector Harlan. "It appears he never arrived at Kradmoor as planned, but that means there's a good chance he still has his memory. He might be able to give us a clue."

That stage magician is the world-famous mesmerist Mysterion the Magnificent whose whereabouts are unknown at this time.

CHAPTER FOUR

Et Tu, Brute?

In which Molly, Timmy, and Ben discover the CENTRAL HIVE only to be betrayed in a life-threatening situation. Twice.

STAY IN *SINGLE FILE* AND KEEP TO THIS *GANGWAY.*

THERE'S NOTHING BUT *HIGHLY CAUSTIC SLUDGE* BELOW US.

HHHHHHAAAAAASSHHHHHHHAAAAFFFFOOOOLLLLAAAAASSSHHHHH

TIMMY.... TIMMY...

THIS WAY, TIMMY.

HHHHHHAAAAAASSHHHHHHHAAAAFFFOOOOLLLLAAAAASSHHHHHH

FOLLOW US, TIMMY.

FOLLOW US, TIMMY.

FOLLOW US, TIMMY.

HEY, IT LOOKS LIKE THE *KID'S* TAKING THE LEAD.

SSHHHHHHHHHAAAA

WAIT UP, TIMMY.

YOU'RE BEAUTIFUL...

WHO YOU *TALKING* TO, KID?

FFFFOOOOLLLAAAAAHHHHHHH

HHHHAAAAASSHHHHHHHHAAAAFFFFOOOOLLLAAAAASSSHHH